MOY MOY

by Leo Politi

Charles Scribner's Sons, New York

To all the Chinese-American Children

Moy Moy and her brothers live on Chanking Street in Los Angeles. There are many brightly colored shops on the street, and one of these belongs to Moy Moy's family.

Peter, Johnny, Tommy and Lily live above this shop with their father and mother.

Lily is never called by her real name. Her brothers call her Moy Moy. In Chinese this means little sister.

Moy Moy's brothers love her very much. When she is tired from playing they carry her home piggy-back.

When the boys go to school
Moy Moy stays home with her mother. Sometimes
she goes to visit her friends the shopkeepers along
the street. She often carries a toy shaped like a large bee.
Buzz goes the bee as Moy Moy swings it around and
around. Then everyone knows she is coming.

Everyone likes Moy Moy. As she goes by they say,

"Nee how mah, Moy Moy?"
"How are you, Moy Moy?"

Moy Moy likes to visit Mr. Fong's shop. The shop is filled with toys. There are puppets, dolls, small pagodas and temples, little flags, drums, swords and trumpets.

Kites hang from the ceiling, and there is a big lantern in the shape of a fantail fish.

As Moy Moy looks around, her eyes are filled with wonder. Before she leaves she always stops to look at the toy she loves best of all—a Chinese doll in a box. Moy Moy knows China is a faraway land where her father and mother lived when they were little.

In the afternoon Moy Moy's brothers go to Chinese school to learn to read and write in Chinese. Chinese writing is done with a brush.

Because the Chinese New Year is coming, the boys are making cards with Happy New Year on them. One of the cards is a surprise for Moy Moy.

It says:

恭 賀 新 年　　妹 妹

Happy New Year Moy Moy

Gung Ho Sun Nin

The brightest hour of the day is after school. Then the children meet to play.

Boys like to spin tops, girls like to play jacks with colored stones. They also play tag, hide-and-seek, and dragon. Dragon is the most fun of all.

The dragon is made by a long line of boys and girls holding on to one another. Dorothy, with a sweater over her head, leads the line. She is the dragon's head and the rest of the children are the body. Moy Moy is the dragon's tail. The children laugh and shout as they run and zig-zag through the street.

As the Chinese New Year is coming, everyone on Chanking Street is getting ready for it.

Now the street is decorated with lanterns and with bright lights. People hang "lay-shee" or good luck money over their doorways. They say this will bring them happiness and wealth all through the year.

The children are excited as they look forward to the big day. Charlie is in charge of the plans for the children's parade. He is a kind and jolly man. He loves the children and the children love him.

Moy Moy sits on Charlie's lap as he tells the children what they are to do. Moy Moy is all eyes as she listens. She is too little to remember the festivities of the year before.

The first thing that Charlie does is to show the boys how to do the lion dance for the children's parade.

The lion's head is covered with bright-colored pieces of silk. The mouth and eyes open and close so that the lion can have different expressions. Sometimes the lion eats or he sleeps. Sometimes he looks happy and sometimes he looks mad.

In the dance the lion jumps about and does many amusing things. He stands on his hind legs, crawls along the pavement, dashes down a hill or scrambles up one. He will even climb to the very top of a ladder if he finds one in his way.

The children are inside the lion and make it move. Peter dances the lion's head. Johnny dances the tail.

At first Moy Moy does not go near because she is afraid it is a real lion.

Charlie does not want her to be afraid, so he takes her by the hand to lead her close to the lion.

"See, Moy Moy," he says. He lets her look underneath to see how Peter holds up the lion's head. Then Moy Moy knows it isn't a real lion and she isn't afraid at all. To show this she puts her head in the lion's mouth. Everyone laughs.

Then Moy Moy gives the lion an orange. It is fun to see the lion throw out the peeling from his mouth. He has such a satisfied expression that everyone laughs again.

At last New Year's Day comes.
All the people greet each other.

"Gung Ho Sun Nin!"
"Happy New Year!"

The boys give Moy Moy the card they have made for her.

恭 賀 新 年　　妹 妹

Happy　　New　　Year　　Moy Moy

Soon the children come together for the parade. The girls wear lovely silk costumes. The boys wear bright costumes with colored bands around their legs. Charlie wears his mandarin suit and is busy getting the parade started. Even the lion is dressed up. He is decorated with trimmings and tassels.

The parade begins. The children with flags walk first. Then comes Moy Moy's brother Tommy, wearing a mask. He teases and leads the mighty lion along the way. The lion is followed by the band, and by girls carrying banners and lanterns.

Moy Moy is at the very end of the parade. She carries a big peacock lantern. She is the smallest child in the parade.

Rat-a-tat, rat-a-tat! Firecrackers are set off from all sides. The noise grows louder and louder, as the lion dances through the streets.

Suddenly the lion pretends he is tired and lies down on the pavement. The children laugh as they watch the expressions on his face. At last he closes his droopy eyes and falls asleep.

But when the music begins to play the lion awakes and and is on his feet and on his way again.

The lion stops to dance in front of each shop. After a short dance he looks up at the lay-shee money hanging in the doorway. Then he opens his huge mouth and swallows it.

All the money the lion collects is used for children's parties, and to buy them toys. This is a New Year's gift from the shopkeepers, because they love the children and want to make them happy.

As the lion comes near Moy Moy's shop she runs upstairs. Mother lets Moy Moy hold out the lay-shee money from the balcony. To tease the lion Moy Moy holds the money up so he cannot reach it. This makes him furious and everyone laughs. The lion pretends to try to climb up the wall. After that he reaches high and swallows the money.

When the parade is over the children have a big party. There are delicious Chinese cookies and candies, and toys for everyone.

Charlie knows which toys the children like and have been wishing for. He gives something to each one.

A story book for Dorothy and a fan for Mary.

A drum for Ronny. A trumpet for Gary. A toy horse for Willy.

Nancy, who likes to play tricks on people, gets a toy snake that springs at you from a box. And Jim has fun with his tiger puppet.

Moy Moy's brothers get kites, for kite flying begins with the New Year. Peter and Johnny have a green dragon kite. It is so big that it will take both of them to fly it.

Now it is Moy Moy's turn. She holds out her little hands and Charlie puts into them—a Chinese doll. It is the doll that she has seen so often in Mr. Fong's toy shop. Moy Moy hugs the doll close. Now it is her very own!

That night the street is crowded. People come from everywhere to see the dragon parade. The street is bright with many lights and with lanterns.

Moy Moy and her brothers watch the parade from the balcony of a friend's house. Her father is in the dragon parade.

The music begins to play and along the street comes a huge dragon. The dragon is so long that the children cannot see where the tail ends. And it is so tall that as it passes the balcony they can reach out and almost touch it.

No wonder it is so tall, it is held up with poles by hundreds of men. Its body moves like waves in a stormy sea.

If Moy Moy had not known it was a make-believe dragon she might have thought it was some strange creature from another world.

Mother tells the children that when she was a little girl in China she saw a dragon parade. The dragon's head was as high as the roof tops. It was held up by three acrobats standing on each other's shoulders.

The children watch with wonder as thousands of firecrackers are set off in the public square. They make bright patterns against the darkness of the night. It is the greatest burst of light and noise Moy Moy has ever heard, and she puts her hands over her ears.

When the festival is over, Moy Moy and her mother and brothers go home. Moy Moy's brothers take turns and carry her piggy-back all the way.

People leaving the street give New Year's greetings to each other.

Everyone says to Moy Moy,

"Gung Ho Sun Nin, Moy Moy!"

"Happy New Year, Moy Moy!"